Quentin Blake

ANGELO

RED FOX

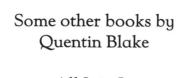

Some other books by Quentin Blake

All Join In
Angel Pavement
Clown
Cockatoos
Fantastic Daisy Artichoke
The Green Ship
Loveykins
Mister Magnolia
Mrs Armitage and the Big Wave
Mrs Armitage on Wheels
Mrs Armitage Queen of the Road
Patrick
Quentin Blake's ABC
A Sailing Boat in the Sky
Simpkin
Snuff
Zagazoo

ANGELO
A RED FOX BOOK 978 1 849 41046 5

First published in Great Britain by Jonathan Cape,
an imprint of Random House Children's Books
A Random House Group Company

Jonathan Cape edition published 1970
Red Fox edition published 2010

1 3 5 7 9 10 8 6 4 2

Red Fox Books are published by Random House Children's Books,
61–63 Uxbridge Road, London W5 5SA

www.kidsatrandomhouse.co.uk
www.rbooks.co.uk

Addresses for companies within The Random House Group Limited can be found at:
www.randomhouse.co.uk/offices.htm

THE RANDOM HOUSE GROUP Limited Reg. No. 954009

A CIP catalogue record for this book is available from the British Library.

Printed in China

This is a story about a boy who lived a long time ago
in Italy. His name was Angelo.

His mother and father went about the country with a horse and cart. With them went Angelo; and his two elder brothers, who were twins, called Beppo and Benno; and his younger brother, who was very small, and who was called Sandro. All their belongings were in the cart.

Whenever they came to a village they stopped their cart in the square, and started to put up a stage. Angelo's father and his big brothers made the stage with planks, and the rest of the family helped to put up curtains and strings of flags.

Then they would pull out the dressing-up basket
and dress up in their costumes. And then the show
began. Soon there was a crowd in the square, and
people looked out from their windows. Angelo's
father banged on a drum, and Beppo and Benno
did marvellous balancing tricks.

They could stand upside-down
on each other's heads, and
were very good at tripping
each other up, and falling over.

After that Angelo's father sang funny songs, and played on the guitar, and Angelo's mother shook her tambourine. Even Sandro had a little drum of his own to bang.

But the most extraordinary thing was Angelo's rope-dancing act. He could climb on to a tight-rope and walk along it.

He could even do a dance on the rope!
And he never fell off. Down below, the people
stared and clapped their hands.

And then in the evening, when they had finished their songs and dances, and had packed up their stage and their costumes, they would go and camp under the trees, and Angelo's mother would cook their dinner. Sometimes Beppo and Benno would juggle with the eggs; and Angelo's father would play to them on the guitar.

And so they travelled about Italy from village to village.

Until one day, when Angelo had just finished his rope-dance, he saw a girl looking at him from a window. But instead of smiling, like everybody else, she had tears running down her face.

"What's the matter?" asked Angelo.

"I wish I could be a rope-dancer and go about the country like you," she said; and then she told Angelo all about herself. The strangest thing of all was her name was Angelina.

Poor Angelina! She had no father or mother and she had to live with her uncle. He was a very mean and gloomy man. He was supposed to look after Angelina, but really she had to look after him. She had to dust the tables and the chairs, and she had to wash the floors – they were enormous.

Then she had to wash the dishes, and wash the clothes . . .

. . . and do all the ironing.

At night she slept in a little hard bed. In her bedroom were two mice she used to talk to, but she hadn't any other friends because her uncle hardly ever allowed her to go out.

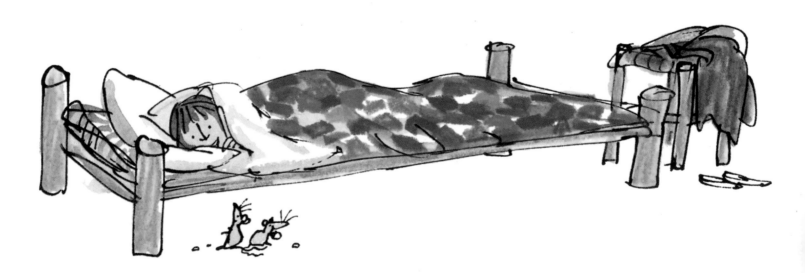

Every night Angelina's uncle
locked all the doors with a
big bunch of keys.

"I wish I could come
away with you," said Angelina.
"But my uncle will keep me
locked up here for ever."

"Never mind," said Angelo.
"I know what to do."

That night, when the streets were empty, Angelo and
his two big brothers crept out with the dressing-up
basket. Angelo stood on Beppo's shoulders; Beppo
stood on Benno's shoulders . . .

. . . Benno stood on the basket; and they just reached the window. Angelina was waiting. They lifted her down, and quickly she hid in the basket.

Off they ran to where the cart was waiting. When the sun rose next morning Angelo's family had gone, and so had Angelina.

After that, Angelina was just like one of the family.
She went with them everywhere in their cart, and
every day Angelo gave her lessons in rope-dancing.
To start with Angelina fell off rather a lot. But in the
end she could really dance on the rope. And then
Angelo's mother made Angelina a beautiful costume
of her own.

And so Angelo and Angelina danced together on the rope, and the people laughed and clapped to see them wherever they went.